KT-447-882

Jack's
Junk

by Elizabeth Dale and Mirella Mariani

W
FRANKLIN WATTS
LONDON•SYDNEY

Jack liked making things with junk.

He asked Mum and Dad to keep things for him.

Whenever Mum had something in a box, she gave it to Jack.

Whenever Dad had something left over, he gave it to Jack.

Mum said it was just junk,

but Jack had lots of fun with it.

Jack wanted to make a tree house.

He got a big box and some newspaper.
He cut and coloured and stuck things
together.

He took it into the garden
and put it in the tree.

But the wind blew
and the house fell out of the tree.
"Never mind," said Jack.
"I can mend it."
And he did.

Then Jack found some string
and tied the box to the tree.
"I am good at mending,"
Jack said to his mum.

"I will make a boat next," said Jack.

He found a lid and some wood.

He hammered and tied

and stuck things together.

"This will be a good boat!" he said.

Jack put the boat on the pond
and gave it a push.

Oh no! The boat did not float.

It started to sink.

"Never mind," said Jack. "I can mend it."

Jack had an idea.

He looked in the junk and found a bag.

Then he stuck it on the hole.

"I am good at mending,"

Jack said to his dad.

Jack's friends came to the house.

"Can Jack come and play

on the go-kart?" they said.

They took the go-kart
to the top of the hill.
One of the children got into the go-kart
and they let it go.
It went faster and faster!

"That looks great fun!" said Jack.

"Can I have a go?"

"I want to go faster," said Jack.

They took the go-kart to

the top of the hill, and pushed it.

It went even faster!

The go-kart went down the hill ...

... and crashed into the wall.

Oh no! The go-kart was broken!

Jack looked at the go-kart.

He had mended the house
and the boat.

Could he mend the go-kart, too?

The children took the go-kart back to Jack's house and Jack set to work.
He cut and folded.

He hammered and tied
and stuck things together.

Soon, the go-kart was fixed.

"I am good at mending things with junk,"

Jack said to his friends.

Story order

Look at these 5 pictures and captions.
Put the pictures in the right order
to retell the story.

1

The go-kart was broken.

2

The go-kart went down the hill.

3

Jack's friends came to the house.

4

Jack likes mending things from junk!

5

Jack collects junk to make things.

Guide for Independent Reading

This series is designed to provide an opportunity for your child to read on their own. These notes are written for you to help your child choose a book and to read it independently.

In school, your child's teacher will often be using reading books which have been banded to support the process of learning to read. Use the book band colour your child is reading in school to help you make a good choice. *Jack's Junk* is a good choice for children reading at Turquoise Band in their classroom to read independently.

The aim of independent reading is to read this book with ease, so that your child enjoys the story and relates it to their own experiences.

About the book

Jack loves making things from junk. But the things he makes don't always work first time. Luckily, Jack is good at mending things, too.

Before reading

Help your child to learn how to make good choices by asking:
"Why did you choose this book? Why do you think you will enjoy it?"
Look at the cover together and ask: "What do you think the story will be about?" Ask your child to think of what they already know about the story context. Then ask your child to read the title aloud.
Ask: "What do you think Jack will be doing in the story?"
Remind your child that they can sound out the letters to make a word if they get stuck.
Decide together whether your child will read the story independently or read it aloud to you.

During reading

Remind your child of what they know and what they can do independently. If reading aloud, support your child if they hesitate or ask for help by telling the word. If reading to themselves, remind your child that they can come and ask for your help if stuck.

After reading

Support comprehension by asking your child to tell you about the story. Use the story order puzzle to encourage your child to retell the story in the right sequence, in their own words. The correct sequence can be found on the next page.

Help your child think about the messages in the book that go beyond the story and ask: "Why do you think Jack likes to fix things? What do you think his friends think of him when he fixes the go-kart?" Give your child a chance to respond to the story: "Did you have a favourite part? What did you think of the things that Jack made?"

Extending learning

Help your child understand the story structure by using the same sentence patterning and adding different elements. "Let's make up a new story about Jack. What other useful things could Jack make from recycled materials? How about something that could fly, or something that helped his parents in the house or garden?"

In the classroom, your child's teacher may be teaching about recognising punctuation marks. Ask your child to identify some question marks and exclamation marks in the story and then ask them to practise reading the whole sentences with appropriate expression.

Franklin Watts
First published in Great Britain in 2018
by The Watts Publishing Group

Series Editors: Jackie Hamley and Melanie Palmer
Series Advisors: Dr Sue Bodman and Glen Franklin
Series Designer: Peter Scoulding

A CIP catalogue record for this book is
available from the British Library.

ISBN 978 1 4451 6213 3 (hbk)
ISBN 978 1 4451 6214 0 (pbk)
ISBN 978 1 4451 6212 6 (library ebook)

Printed in China

Franklin Watts
An imprint of
Hachette Children's Group
Part of The Watts Publishing Group
Carmelite House
50 Victoria Embankment
London EC4Y 0DZ

An Hachette UK Company
www.hachette.co.uk

www.franklinwatts.co.uk

Answer to Story order: 5, 3, 2, 1, 4